THUNDERBIRDS™

FAB ANNUAL 2003

STEPHEN COLE

CARLTON
BOOKS

THIS IS A CARLTON BOOK

Published by Carlton Books Limited 2002
20 Mortimer Street
London W1T 3JW

A CIP catalogue for this book is available from the British Library

ISBN 1 84222 675 4

Editor: Claire Richardson
Design: Tony Fleetwood
Production: Lisa French

Calling International Rescue!

The year is 2065. The place is … anywhere an emergency call might take them. It could be a doomed spaceship heading straight for the sun, an oil-rig collapsing into the blazing sea, a rogue satellite plummeting from the skies to destroy a massive refinery.

The very fact that you are reading this means you have been granted top-level security clearance and are deemed a friend of International Rescue. This secret dossier I have prepared contains all you need to know about the organization and the amazing technology, not to mention special agents, at its command. It's a story of courage, of skill and, perhaps most importantly, of the vision of one very special man – the founder of International Rescue, Jeff Tracy.

Lady Penelope Creighton-Ward

CONTENTS

The Secrets of Tracy Island

As you already know, International Rescue is a secret independent organization dedicated to assisting in crisis situations where conventional methods have proved inadequate. When disasters occur, whether as the result of a natural accident or some technological breakdown, it is never long before one of the Thunderbird craft arrives on the scene. But where do they come from?

The answer lies hidden somewhere in the Southern Pacific Ocean. Tracy Island is owned by retired multi-millionaire Jeff Tracy, who lives there with his family and a number of helpers. Having made a fortune through his incredible construction and engineering skills, Jeff then put his talents to even better use, masterminding the

Round House

When the main house is full, the Tracys' guests can be accommodated in this luxury alternative. What they will never guess, though, is that beneath them are the hangar and launch bay for Thunderbird 3, which rises vertically through the hollow centre of the house.

Tracy Villa

Built into the cliff face, this large two-storey building looks like any luxury home, with its swimming pool and wonderful views of the island. Inside, however, it has been adapted so that Jeff can direct operations from his desk in the lounge. From here his sons can also access their various craft.

formation of International Rescue. Aware that the amazing craft at International Rescue's disposal had to remain top secret, he worked with the genius inventor known only as Brains to conceal the Thunderbird vessels beneath his idyllic island home. Few know the precise location of Tracy Island and fewer still would ever guess that it houses International Rescue's headquarters

Thunderbird 1 Hangar

The swimming pool on the patio has been cleverly adapted so that it can slide back to reveal Thunderbird 1's hangar and launch bay.

Cliff House

Overlooking the island's runway, the house also has stunning views out to sea.

Thunderbird 2 Hangar

Located behind a hidden door cut into the rock under the Cliff House is the enormous hangar that houses Thunderbird 2 and its six detachable pods. It also contains a workshop area and specialist rescue equipment.

Launch Ramp

When Thunderbird 2 is ready to launch, the palm trees lining the runway fall away and a section of the runway itself is raised by hydraulics to an angle of 45 degrees. A blast barrier prevents damage to the runway from the craft's incredible rocket thrusters.

REPORT FILED BY

JEFF TRACY

Jeff Tracy here. They say you can't stand in the way of progress...that one day computers will do everything for us. But when it comes to bravery, skill and guts, a human being cannot be replaced – as we all discovered during a daring space station rescue...

IT WAS JUST ANOTHER ROUTINE ROCKET LAUNCH AT SENTINEL BASE...

THE AUTOMATED SYSTEMS WERE HANDLING EVERYTHING...

ALL THE STAFF HAD TO DO WAS WATCH.

IT WAS A FAR CRY FROM THE WAY WE DID THINGS IN MY DAY, AS I TOLD THE BOYS...

I REMEMBER ONE TIME, THE ROCKET WAS EXPERIMENTAL...HEY, TIN-TIN!...

...TURN THE VOLUME DOWN, WILL YOU?

BUT IT'S MICHELLE AND THE ASTEROIDS! THEY'RE GREAT!

AND THAT'S IT FOR TODAY'S SHOW WITH YOURS TRULY, RICK O'SHEA!

TIN-TIN HAD A SOFT SPOT FOR THE DJ.

ISN'T HE JUST MINTY!

I CAN'T SEE ANYTHING IN HIM MYSELF.

YOU'RE JEALOUS!

WHY SHOULD I BE JEALOUS OF THAT CLOWN?

YOU'RE ALL OVERLOOKING ONE IMPORTANT POINT. THOSE TV-CASTS ARE COMING FROM AN UNAUTHORIZED SPACE STATION.

MILLIONS OF SATELLITES ORBIT THE WORLD IN AN EXACT, INTERNATIONALLY PLANNED PATH. BUT O'SHEA'S SPACE STATION WAS NOT CONTROLLED...

IT WAS A MENACE!

MEANWHILE, THE LAUNCH AT SENTINEL BASE WAS GOING AHEAD.

STAGE TWO OF THE SEPARATION WENT WITHOUT A HITCH...

STAGE 3

STAGE 2

BUT THEN THE EMERGENCY ALARM WENT OFF.

THE COMPUTER REPORTED THAT THE ROCKET WAS OUT OF CONTROL. IT WOULD HAVE TO BE DESTROYED.

INTERNATIONAL SPACE CONTROL STUDIED THE ROCKET'S COURSE AND CALCULATED A SAFE PLACE TO DETONATE.

AREA REFERENCE A4 – DESTRUCTION ALTITUDE 128 MILES –

BUT NO ONE REALIZED THAT O'SHEA AND HIS ASSISTANT, LOMAN, WERE IN THAT EXACT AREA OF SPACE.

...CLOSE TO THE UNAUTHORIZED SPACE STATION.

THE ROCKET EXPLODED...

WHAT HAPPENED?

O'SHEA...YOU ALL RIGHT?

SOME SORT OF EXPLOSION. I SHOULD GO OUTSIDE TO CHECK THE DAMAGE.

AS LONG AS WE'RE IN ONE PIECE, THE SHOW GOES ON.

MEANWHILE, THUNDERBIRD 3 DISENGAGED FROM THUNDERBIRD 5 AFTER ROUTINE MAINTENANCE TO A MONITOR.

IT'LL BE THREE HOURS BEFORE IT'S OPERATIONAL.

LET'S HOPE OUR ASSISTANCE IS NOT REQUIRED.

BUT, UNBEKNOWN TO US, IT SOON WOULD BE...

THE EXPLOSION HAD KNOCKED O'SHEA'S SPACE STATION OUT OF ORBIT.

WE'RE HEADING FOR EARTH RE-ENTRY – AND ANNIHILATION.

THE BRAKING PARACHUTES HAD MALFUNCTIONED.

THERE'S NOTHING TO SLOW US DOWN...

LOMAN DECIDED TO SPACEWALK OUTSIDE TO INSPECT THE DAMAGE.

9

THUNDERBIRDS ARE GO!

THUNDERBIRD 3 RACED TO THE RESCUE.

WE'RE APPROXIMATELY THREE MINUTES AWAY.

WHEN WE'RE IN POSITION, OPEN THE OUTER AIRLOCK DOOR.

ONCE AGAIN, ALAN MADE THE DARING JOURNEY TO THE SPACE STATION'S AIRLOCK.

I'M GOING TO CUT THROUGH THE DOOR. MAKE SURE YOUR SPACESUIT'S ON CORRECTLY.

I...I CAN'T DO IT! I'D RATHER TAKE MY CHANCES IN HERE!

SCOTT, O'SHEA'S CHICKENING OUT!

THERE'S VERY LITTLE TIME. IF YOU CROSS AFTER RE-ENTRY, WIND RESISTANCE WILL RIP YOU TO PIECES!

ALAN GOT TO WORK WITH HIS CUTTING TOOL.

CLOSE THE OUTER DOOR, O'SHEA. I'M COMING IN!

INTERNATIONAL SPACE CONTROL LEARNED OF OUR INVOLVEMENT.

WE HAVE RADAR CONTACT WITH THE SPACE STATION. IT'S HEADING FOR THE OIL INSTALLATION AT A'BEN DUH!

THAT'S JUST ABOUT THE BIGGEST REFINERY IN THE MIDDLE EAST!

WE KNEW THE IMPACT WOULD CAUSE WIDESPREAD DAMAGE AND TERRIBLE FIRES.

HOW DO WE TACKLE THIS ONE, BRAINS?

THE SPACE STATION WAS STARTING TO BREAK UP.

BRAINS WENT TO THE MISSILE TURRET, READY TO BLAST THE SPACE STATION OUT OF THE SKY.

BUT THEN VIRGIL HEARD AN UNEXPECTED BROADCAST.

IT'S O'SHEA! HE MUST STILL BE ON BOARD!

WITH THUNDERBIRD 5 OUT OF ACTION, VIRGIL AND BRAINS COULDN'T CONTACT ME FOR ADVICE

O'SHEA OR THE REFINERY?

IT'S ONE LIFE AGAINST MANY, VIRGIL.

I THINK WE CAN TILT THE SPACECRAFT OFF COURSE, TO CRASH IN THE DESERT.

USING THUNDERBIRD 2 AS A KIND OF BUMPER CAR!

YOU'RE RIGHT. THE PERSONNEL AT THE REFINERY MUST COME FIRST.

... WITH BREATHTAKING SKILL, VIRGIL GOT THUNDERBIRD 2 INTO POSITION.

...AND STEERED THE SPACE STATION AWAY.

THE REFINERY WAS SAVED!

AND THE SPACE STATION CRASHED HARMLESSLY INTO THE DESERT.

THUNDERBIRD 2

POOR O'SHEA. BUT WHAT COULD WE DO?

WITH HEAVY HEARTS, VIRGIL AND BRAINS CAME HOME TO JOIN US.

THE LESSON'S BEEN LEARNED, FATHER. YOU WON'T FIND ANOTHER PIRATE STATION WANTING TO GO INTO ORBIT.

VIRGIL AND BRAINS WERE SURPRISED TO SEE US SO CHEERFUL.

UNLESS THEY GET AUTHORITY FROM INTERNATIONAL SPACE CONTROL.

O'SHEA WAS...KILLED.

YOU'VE GOT IT ALL WRONG, BOYS. HE'S AS ALIVE AS I AM.

BUT WE HEARD HIS VOICE BROADCASTING!

I THINK I KNOW WHAT MUST'VE HAPPENED...

Braman's Brain

Brains has built some special components that he hopes will make his robotic creation Braman think more quickly than ever. But now Brains is away with Virgil on a special mission and Braman's incredible computing power is needed. Help Gordon put the parts in place by drawing lines to match each component to its own specially designed socket in Braman's brain.

(Solutions on page 60)

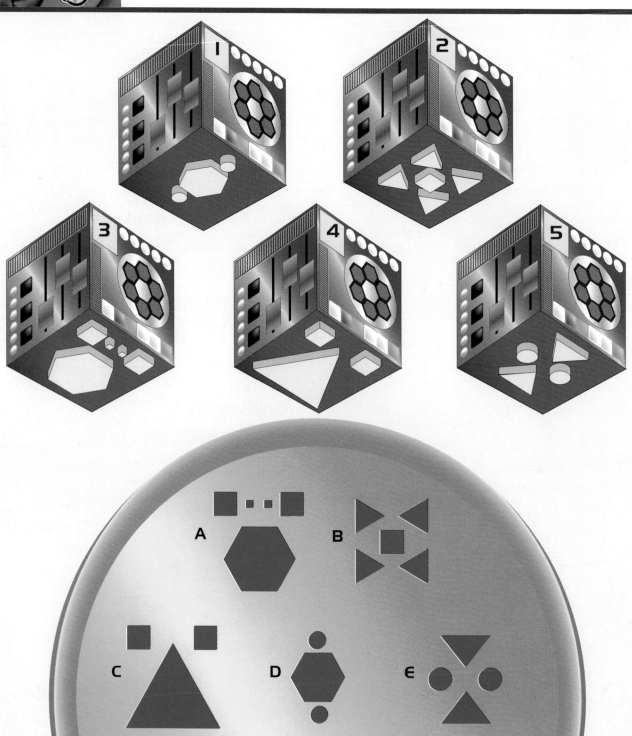

Thunderbird I and Scott Tracy

Craft and Crew

The Craft

Name: Thunderbird I
Top speed: 15,000 m.p.h.
Length: 115 feet
Wing span: 80 feet
Fuel: Main drives powered atomically.
Purpose: To reach the danger zone swiftly so that Scott can advise on precisely what other International Rescue hardware and personnel will be needed.
Special features include: Ultra-high-frequency guidance system, sonar sounding equipment, destructor cannon.

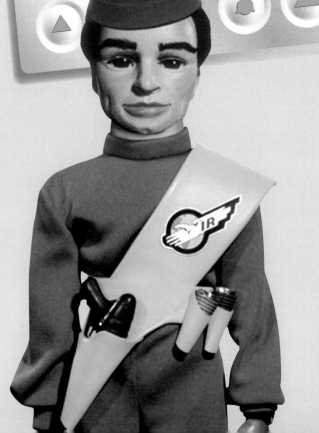

Craft and Crew

The Pilot

Name: Scott Tracy
Age: 26
Education: Yale and Oxford universities
Character: Brave, quick-thinking, fast-talking, confident.
Other duties include: Co-piloting Thunderbird 3, commanding International Rescue in Jeff Tracy's absence.
Status: F.A.B.!

Know Your Enemy: The Hood

As an affiliated agent of International Rescue, it is your duty to report any sighting of the organization's enemies. And right at the top of the "Most Wanted" list is the evil Hood…

Name: The Hood
Known aliases: Agent 79, Codename 671
Age: 47
Distinguishing features: Glowing, hypnotic eyes; broad, bald head; wide, flat nose; bushy eyebrows (but see also **Special powers** below).
Aim: To amass vast personal wealth – no matter what the cost to others.
HQ: A mysterious temple hidden in the Malaysian jungle
Origins: The Hood is the half-brother of Kyrano, who runs the Tracy household. He was brought up in Malaya, where he cheated Kyrano out of his rightful inheritance of their father's estate and riches. Kyrano turned his back on material gain as a result of his half-brother's treachery, but to the Hood, money and the power it brings, became his obsession.
Special powers: The Hood is so called because of his gift for adopting uncannily convincing disguises that enable him to move among his enemies without their knowledge. He can also hypnotize people and uses his special powers against his enemies – sometimes with deadly results.
Danger rating: Maximum. The Hood knows that the secrets of the Thunderbird craft could make him rich beyond even *his* wildest dreams and he will stop at nothing to achieve his goal.

Recent sightings

1. Outside London, having sabotaged the maiden flight of the atomic-powered aircraft Fireflash.

2. Attempting to spy on an atomic irrigation plant in Australia.

3. Causing sabotage at another atomic irrigation plant in the Sahara desert.

4. Secretly filming an International Rescue attempt in the Nevada desert.

5. Stealing top-security research documents from a satellite tracking station in the Northern Territory of Australia

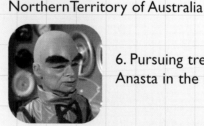
6. Pursuing treasure at Lake Anasta in the Middle East.

Who knows…maybe this arch-villain will appear next somewhere near YOU!

Agent briefing

To help you become familiar with the Hood's natural appearance, you must complete the following exercises!

1. Broken Image

Carefully copy the picture here into the space beside it. The grid will help you to copy more accurately.

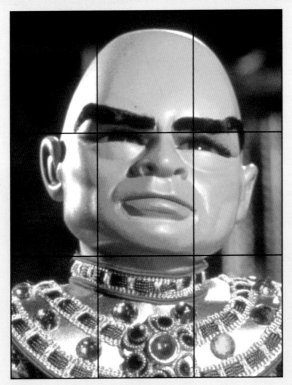

2. ID Parade

You must be able to recognize the Hood from all angles and spot his preferred costume at a glance. Using the first picture as reference, colour in the other two pictures.

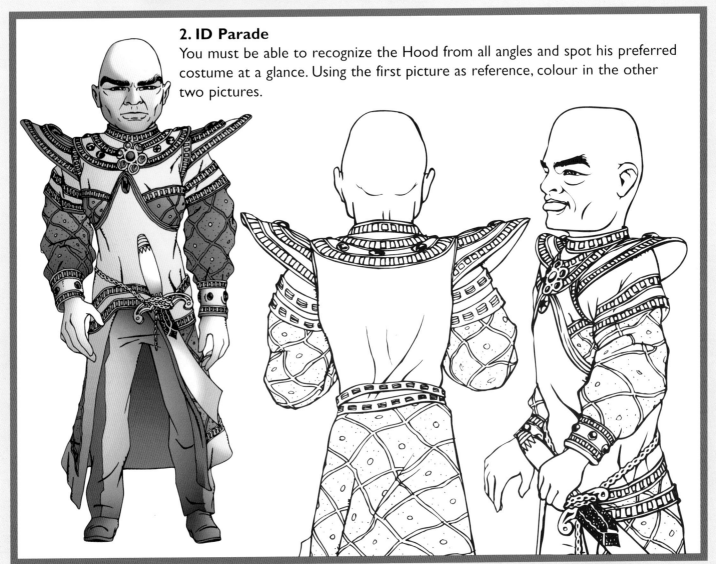

REPORT FILED BY
JEFF TRACY

Being in charge of International Rescue is a full-time job. An emergency call could come through at any time. Even when I do take a vacation, I'm soon glad to get back to work. I recall one time...

IT ALL STARTED WHEN LADY PENELOPE INVITED ME TO STAY AT HER FARM IN BONGA-BONGA IN AUSTRALIA.

YOU HAVEN'T HAD A HOLIDAY IN AT LEAST EIGHTEEN MONTHS!

RELUCTANTLY I AGREED.

SCOTT, YOU'RE NEXT IN LINE. YOU'LL HAVE TO TAKE MY PLACE WHILE I'M AWAY.

MEANWHILE, THE WORLD NAVY WERE ON MANOEUVRES IN THE ATLANTIC.

THERE'S NO CHANCE OF ANY DANGER.

I HOPE YOU'RE RIGHT!

ALERT ALL VESSELS IN VICINITY. AND WARN THE DRILLING RIG SEASCAPE!

PREPARE TO TEST GYROPEDOES. THESE NEW WEAPONS COULD REVOLUTIONIZE UNDERSEA FIREPOWER.

IN THE NAVY'S ATOM SUB...

GYROPEDOES READY TO LAUNCH...

SEEK AND DESTROY!

THE FIRST MISSILE FOUND ITS DUMMY TARGET...

BUT THE SECOND MISSILE WAS OUT OF CONTROL!

IT HIT THE SEABED AND EXPLODED – IGNITING A GAS FIELD!

MEANWHILE, I HAD ARRIVED AT LADY PENELOPE'S FARM IN BONGA-BONGA...

I'D FEEL BETTER IF I COULD CHECK IN WITH THE BOYS...

TRY TO FORGET ALL ABOUT INTERNATIONAL RESCUE!

JOHN WAS MONITORING THE SITUATION IN THE ATLANTIC FROM THUNDERBIRD 5 AND WARNED SCOTT...

THERE'S A MASSIVE JET OF FIRE BLAZING UP THIRTY MILES FROM THE RIG!

24

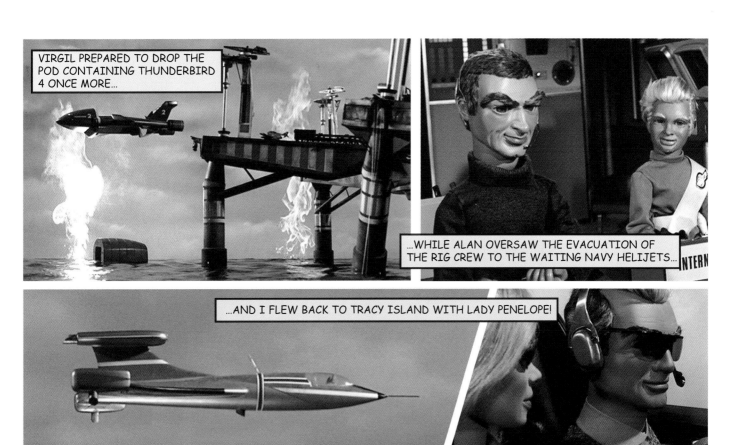

VIRGIL PREPARED TO DROP THE POD CONTAINING THUNDERBIRD 4 ONCE MORE...

...WHILE ALAN OVERSAW THE EVACUATION OF THE RIG CREW TO THE WAITING NAVY HELIJETS...

...AND I FLEW BACK TO TRACY ISLAND WITH LADY PENELOPE!

THE RIG WAS STARTING TO BREAK UP. DEBRIS WAS SINKING TO THE SEA BED.

THEY'LL NEVER GET US OUT...NOT WITH ALL THAT METAL ON TOP OF US!

I'LL HAVE TO CUT THROUGH THE GUIDE CABLES HOLDING THE SPHERE TO THE SUPPORT COLUMN!

THE WORK WAS PAINSTAKING AND SLOW...

Lady Penelope Puzzles It Out!

After a night spent drinking with some old friends from Parkmoor Scrubs Prison, Parker got his hands (and don't ask me how, because I don't want to know!) on some very strange papers. At first they seemed merely mysterious, but on closer inspection we realized that they were vital to foiling a fiendish plot against Jeff and the boys!

The first piece of paper, outlining the simple aim of the gang in code, is reproduced below:

> DESTROY TOIL SECURE
> I.R. ANTENNA
>
> DESTROY EAT RICE, SOAR
> IN TUNNEL
>
> DESTROY USE ALIEN TIN
> CREATOR "N"

We soon realized that each of the three sentences contained the same selection of blue letters, arranged in a different order. In each case they form an anagram which unscrambles to reveal the same two words — words we know very well…Can you unscramble the anagrams? And can you make any more anagrams out of the letters in blue?

> The biggest clue was h'in the first sentence…

The second piece of paper held the details of the cunning plot! It was a plan to kidnap five key members of Jeff's team and hold them hostage…By studying the paper closely, reading along letter by letter, I was able to find the names of the gang's victims hidden in the message in time. Can you?

> WE WILL MEET AT ASCOT TODAY AT 2100. THE TARGETS EITHER DO NOT SUSPECT OUR GANG OR DO NOT WISH US TO KNOW THEY SUSPECT. AS A PRECAUTION, TAKE NO PART IN TINKERING WITH OUR SECRET PLANS BEFORE THE FINAL BRAINSTORMING SESSION. THIS IS MY FINAL ANNOUNCEMENT!

> Check your h'answers on page 60!

Brains's Birthdays

Brains has an amazing memory for scientific facts and figures, but he's not so good at remembering birthdays – even his own! He programmed his friends' special days into a computational grid, but now a power surge has left the information scrambled! Can you find all the birth-dates in the grid below? Search backwards and forwards, in straight lines up, down and across.

BRAINS
14-11-2040

PARKER
30-05-2013

TIN-TIN
20-06-2043

JEFF
02-01-2009

SCOTT
04-04-2039

VIRGIL
15-08-2041

ALAN
12-03-2044

JOHN
08-10-2040

0	4	0	4	2	0	3	9	2	0
3	0	8	2	0	4	2	0	2	3
4	2	1	4	1	1	2	0	4	0
0	1	0	2	2	5	4	7	4	0
2	7	2	0	2	0	3	7	0	5
6	9	0	7	4	8	3	5	2	2
0	1	4	0	2	2	0	4	3	0
0	2	0	1	2	0	0	9	0	1
2	2	0	1	2	4	2	2	2	3
9	3	0	2	2	1	4	2	1	0

Work out the birthdays, fill in the boxes and find these birth-dates in the grid too!

LADY PENELOPE

☐☐ ☐☐ ☐☐☐☐

GORDON

☐☐ ☐☐ ☐☐☐☐

(See page 60 for Solutions)

OH MY, BRAMAN. I'VE, UH, FORGOTTEN LADY PENELOPE'S AND GORDON'S BIRTHDAYS! CAN YOU HELP ME OUT SO I CAN WRITE THEM IN THIS GRID MATRIX?

LADY PENELOPE'S BIRTHDAY IS CHRISTMAS EVE. SHE IS FIVE YEARS OLDER THAN ALAN. GORDON'S BIRTHDAY IS VALENTINE'S DAY. HE IS THIRTY YEARS YOUNGER THAN PARKER.

Thunderbird 2 and Virgil Tracy

Craft and Crew

The Craft

Name: Thunderbird 2
Length: 250 feet
Wing span: 180 feet
Top speed: 5,000 m.p.h.
Purpose: Carries rescue equipment to scene of disaster in detachable pods.
Fuel: Atomic pile powers turbo jets to rear for cruising and rocket thrusters for take-off and landing.
Special features include: cutting tools, drills, lasers, missiles.

Craft and Crew

The Pilot

Name: Virgil Tracy
Age: 24
Education: Denver School of Advanced Technology
Character: Daring, mature, artistic.
Other duties include: Operating many of the specialized rescue vehicles that are transported in Thunderbird 2's pods.
Status: F.A.B!

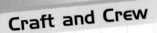

Pick of the Pods

Agent briefing

Whatever the emergency, you can bet there's a pod vehicle to handle it. They can be carried to the danger zone by Thunderbird 2, but each of these mighty machines is useless without Virgil's special skills of observation and judgement. Study the amazing machines on this page, then fit the words in red into the special grid below!

The Mole
A 30-ton jet-propelled drilling machine that can cut through any surface as if it's paper. It's a boring machine that's certainly never boring!

The Excavator
Ploughing a path through the most stubborn rubble, the Excavator chews up rock at one end and then just spits it out at the other!

The Firefly
Whenever fires are raging, the heat-resistant Firefly can be called upon to snuff out the flames with ease!

The Elevator Cars
These twelve-wheeled cars are designed to manoeuvre beneath damaged aircraft and cushion their landings – incredible suspension at times of incredible suspense!

Transmitter Truck
This amazing vehicle is capable of transmitting a signal over 90 million miles through space!

The Monobrake
A vehicle designed for use on monorail lines, its powers of search-and-recovery are a real discovery!

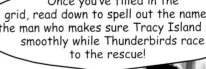

Once you've filled in the grid, read down to spell out the name of the man who makes sure Tracy Island runs smoothly while Thunderbirds race to the rescue!

Craft and Crew

Thunderbird 3 and Alan Tracy

Craft and Crew

The Craft

Name: Thunderbird 3
Length: 287 feet
Nacelle span: 80 feet
Escape velocity: 25,200 m.p.h.
Purpose: For rescue operations in space, and for ferrying personnel and parts to Thunderbird 5.
Fuel: Atomic pile for main drive, rocket propellant for thrusters.
Special features include: transmitters, sophisticated space sensors, spacewalk gear.

Craft and Crew

The Pilot

Name: Alan Tracy
Age: 21
Education: Colorado University
Character: Sporty, resourceful, a practical joker.
Other duties include: Taking turns with John Tracy to man Thunderbird 5.
Status: F.A.B.!

Monobrake Maze

A monotrain has been derailed deep in a mountain tunnel. There are no casualties, but sections of the tunnel are starting to collapse. To reach and rescue the passengers, Virgil must steer the Monobrake through the maze of dark passageways. Using a piece of string to measure the passages, can you work out the fastest route for him to take? Remember, he dare not try to push through a rockfall for fear of causing further cave-ins! (See page 60 for Solutions)

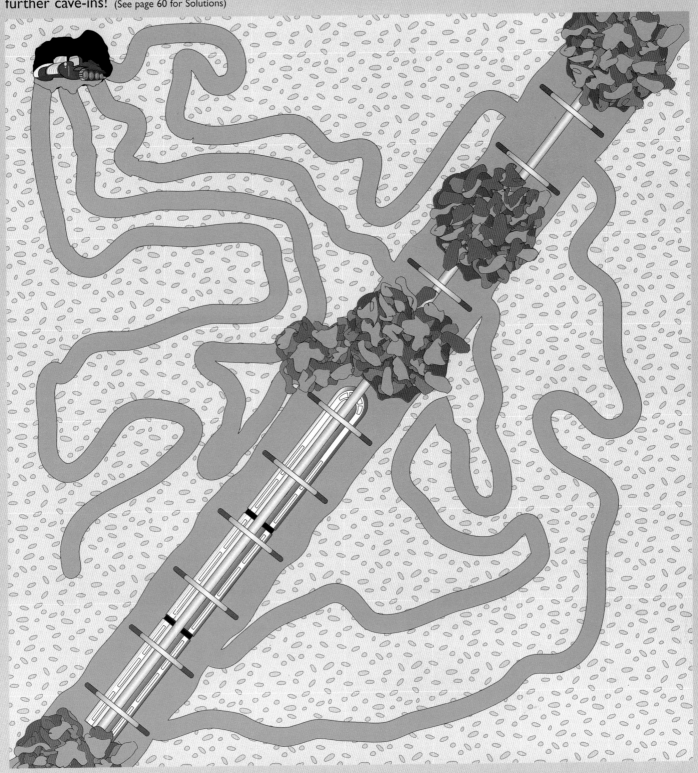

REPORT FILED BY
JOHN TRACY

Monitoring world events from Thunderbird 5, I can tell you that the vacuum of space is a cold, cold place to be. But when a probe was launched to gather matter from the sun, everyone at International Rescue found things in space almost too hot to handle...

AT CAPE KENNEDY, THE SUN PROBE WAS READY FOR TAKE-OFF.

SOLAR CONTROL CENTRE TO ALL PERSONNEL...

GROUND CHECKS COMPLETE. SOLARNAUTS EMBARKED.

FIVE... FOUR...THREE... TWO...ONE!

FULL POWER!

LIFT-OFF! PROJECT SUN PROBE IS ON!

41

43

OPERATING SAFETY BEAM NOW.

BUT THE BEAM WAS TOO WEAK!

WE'LL HAVE TO GO MUCH CLOSER TO THE SUN THAN WE ESTIMATED! WE CAN'T ABANDON THOSE GUYS!

MEANWHILE, THUNDERBIRD 2 HAD REACHED THE HIMALAYAS - THE IDEAL LOCATION FROM WHICH TO BEAM ITS RADIO SIGNAL.

WE'VE TOUCHED DOWN ON MOUNT ARKAN, FATHER. WE'RE ABOUT TO GO OUT IN THE TRANSMITTER TRUCK.

I HOPE THEY HAVE MORE SUCCESS THAN ALAN AND SCOTT.

...AND VIRGIL STEERED IT THROUGH THE FROZEN LANDSCAPE.

THE TRANSMITTER TRUCK ROLLED OUT OF THUNDERBIRD 2...

BUT WHILE THE SUN PROBE WAS NOW SAFE, THUNDERBIRD 3 WAS IN BIG TROUBLE!

OK, THE SOLAR SHIP'S OUT OF DANGER. LET'S HEAD FOR HOME. FIRING RETROS.

RETROS AREN'T WORKING! WE'RE STILL ON A COLLISION COURSE FOR THE SUN!

THE SAFETY BEAM... THAT WOULD CUT THE POWER TO THE RETROS. TIN-TIN, HAVE YOU SHUT DOWN THE BEAM?

BUT TIN-TIN HAD PASSED OUT WITH THE SAFETY BEAM STILL TRANSMITTING. THE SHIP WAS PARALYSED!

I'M COMING DOWN...MUST MAKE IT...SO HOT...

DAD HEARD THE BAD NEWS ON THE TELECAST.

I WON'T BELIEVE IT...I JUST CAN'T! WE MUST GET ON TO BRAINS STRAIGHT AWAY!

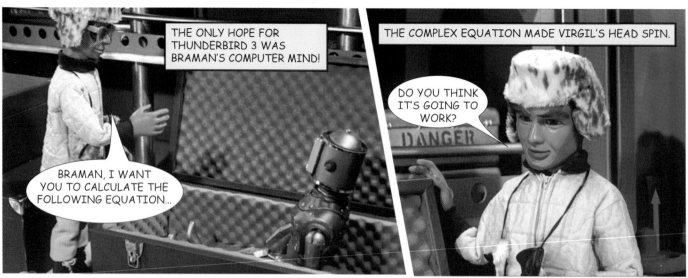

AT LAST, THE TRANSMITTER TRUCK JAMMED THUNDERBIRD 3'S RADIO SIGNAL...

...AND THE RETRO ROCKETS FIRED. ALAN AND HIS CREW WERE SAVED!

HEY...WE'RE MOVING AWAY FROM THE SUN!

SOON I WAS MONITORING THUNDERBIRD 3 ON ITS WAY SAFELY BACK TO EARTH.

I'M REALLY PROUD OF MY INTERNATIONAL RESCUE TEAM TODAY. HEAD BACK FOR BASE, THUNDERBIRDS!

SO, WITH THE HELP OF BRAINS...

...AND HIS PET PROJECT, BRAMAN...

...INTERNATIONAL RESCUE PROVED ONCE AGAIN THAT IT CAN ALWAYS KEEP ITS COOL...NO MATTER WHAT THE TEMPERATURE!

Turnaround Trouble

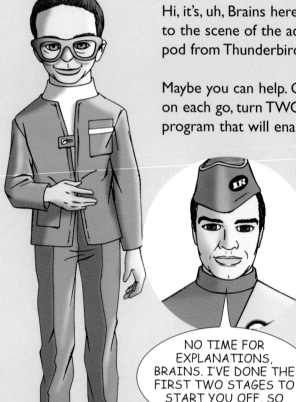

Hi, it's, uh, Brains here. A distress call has been picked up, so Virgil and I have rushed to the scene of the action. But now a circuit has jammed and Virgil can't release the pod from Thunderbird 2!

Maybe you can help. Changing just one letter at a time and spelling out a real word on each go, turn TWO into POD in just three stages. From that I can run a program that will enable the transponders to –

NO TIME FOR EXPLANATIONS, BRAINS. I'VE DONE THE FIRST TWO STAGES TO START YOU OFF, SO GOOD LUCK!

```
T W O
T O O
T O P
_ _ _
P O D
```

Thanks for that. But sadly, no sooner had we lowered the pod and deployed the Domo to hold up a crumbling wall than the entire building collapsed! Now we need the Mole to burrow through to the survivors. But once again the circuits in the pod are jammed.

We need your help a second time! Can you turn DOMO into MOLE by changing just one letter at a time and spelling out a real word on each go? If you can, then we will be able to get through to all those trapped people.

(Solutions on page 60)

WE NEED YOUR HELP AGAIN, AND QUICKLY!

```
D O M O
D O M E
_ _ _ _
_ _ _ _
M O L E
```

Thunderbird 4 and Gordon Tracy

Craft and Crew

The Craft

Name: Thunderbird 4
Length: 30 feet
Wing span: Not applicable
Top speed: Unknown – but fast
Purpose: Underwater and sea surface rescue.
Fuel: Atomic generators for undersea propulsion, nuclear pile at rear for surface speed.
Special features: Battering ram, missiles, electromagnet, laser cutter.

Craft and Crew

The Pilot

Name: Gordon Tracy
Age: 22
Education: A highly trained aquanaut and expert in oceanography
Character: Good-natured, high-spirited, practical.
Other duties: Co-piloting Thunderbird 2, on occasion with Virgil.
Status: F.A.B.!

Transmitter Tangles

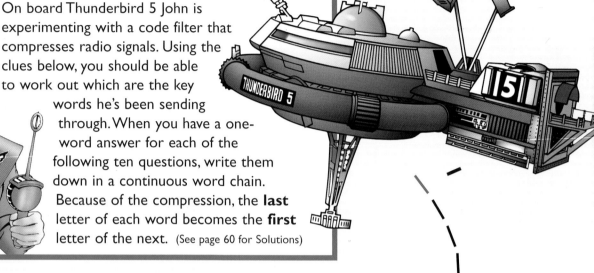

On board Thunderbird 5 John is experimenting with a code filter that compresses radio signals. Using the clues below, you should be able to work out which are the key words he's been sending through. When you have a one-word answer for each of the following ten questions, write them down in a continuous word chain. Because of the compression, the **last** letter of each word becomes the **first** letter of the next. (See page 60 for Solutions)

1 Lady Penelope's trusty chauffeur.

2 Calling International _____!

3 The Thunderbird craft are the fastest vehicles on _____.

4 Jeff is always ready to respond to any cry for ____.

5 The colour of Lady Penelope's Rolls-Royce.

6 Tin-Tin's father and Jeff's old friend.

7 Thunderbird 5 hovers over the world in geostationary _____ .

8 _____s are go!

9 This heavy-duty rescue equipment is built like a tank with three powerful suction pads on its jointed arms.

10 The colour of Thunderbird 3.

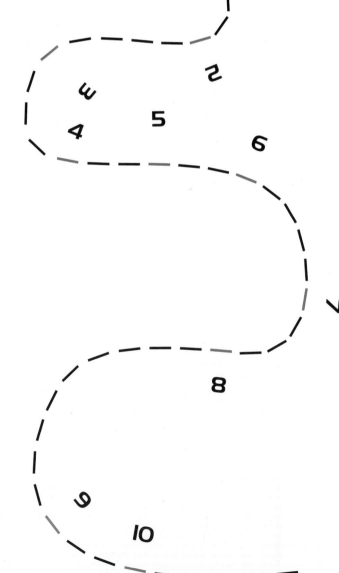

Craft and Crew

Thunderbird 5 and John Tracy

Craft and Crew

The Craft

Name: Thunderbird 5
Length: Classified – but this satellite is truly vast.
Wing span: Not applicable
Top speed: Stationary in orbit above Earth.
Purpose: Scans Earth and space for distress signals, and keeps all Thunderbird craft and personnel in constant contact.
Fuel: Atomic batteries power life-support and monitoring equipment.

Craft and Crew

The Pilot

Name: John Tracy
Age: 25
Education: Harvard University
Character: Quiet, intellectual, precise.
Other duties include: Undertaking important astronomical work from Thunderbird 5.
Status: F.A.B.!

Unidentified F.A.B. Objects!

Brains has invented a device that ruins any photograph taken of a vehicle used by International Rescue. Only trained operatives should be able to recognize these craft from the spoilt pictures. Can you? (See page 60 for Solutions)

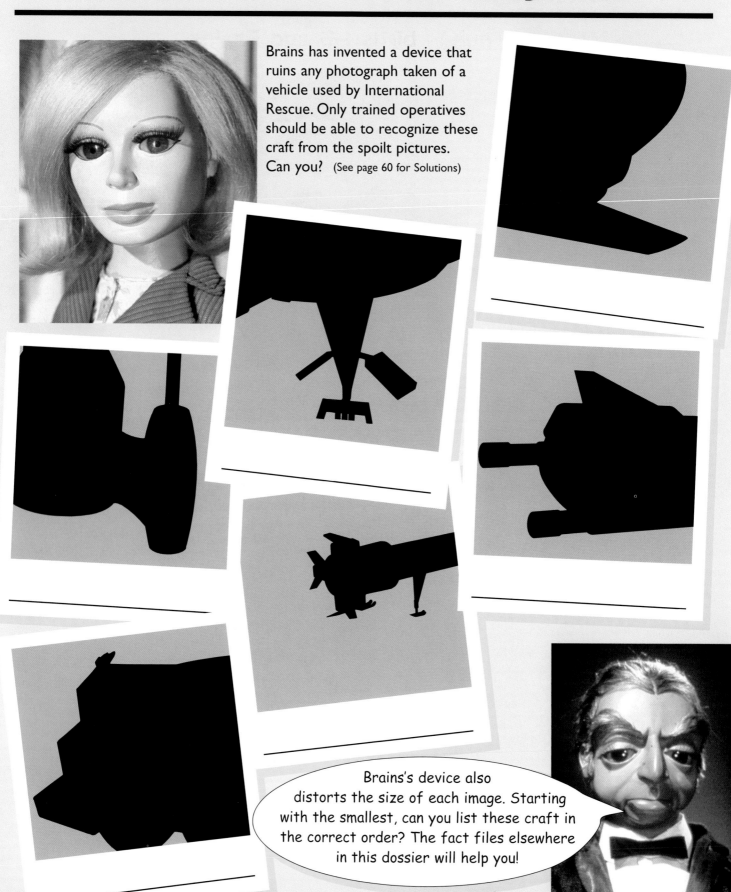

Brains's device also distorts the size of each image. Starting with the smallest, can you list these craft in the correct order? The fact files elsewhere in this dossier will help you!

Thunderbirds 1–5 and Brains

Craft and Creator
The Craft

Though not in charge of any one vehicle, Brains invented all the incredible technology used by International Rescue and is responsible for its safe operation and maintenance. His value to the organization is therefore enormous!

Craft and Creator
The Creator

Name: Brains (real name unknown)
Alias: Hiram K. Hackenbacker
Age: 25
Education: Unknown, but Brains's genius was noticed and encouraged by his adoptive father, who was a professor at Cambridge University.
Character: Quiet, inventive, perfectionist.
Other duties include: Helping on rescue missions (often with Virgil in Thunderbird 2), continually working to improve his inventions and developing technology for outside companies that will enhance human life in the twenty-first century.
Status: F-F-F.A.B.!

Under Sea, Under Pressure!

A group of aquanauts is in danger. The winch cable of their diving sphere has snapped and they have plummeted to the bottom of the inky-black sea. Gordon must act quickly if he is to save them. Help him by carefully following these twisted undersea cables to find out which leads to the diving sphere, so he can tow it to safety! (See page 60 for Solutions)

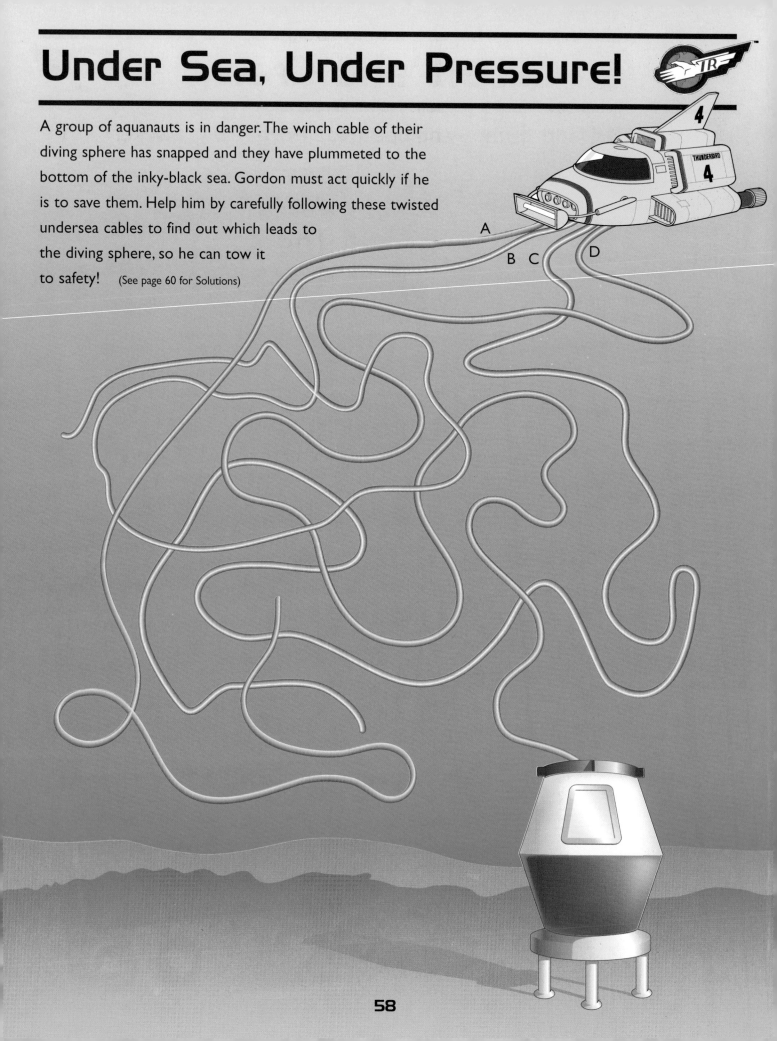

FAB I and Lady Penelope (Not Forgetting Parker!)

Craft and Crew

The Craft

Name: FAB I
Top speed: 200 m.p.h. plus
Length: 21 feet
Wheels: Six
Fuel: Power unit in bonnet.
Purpose: To transport Lady Penelope – and her many secret gadgets and weapons – over land and sea in maximum safety.
Special features include: Machine guns at front and rear, lasers, smoke bombs and oil-slick generators, booster jets and skis for snowy conditions.

Craft and Crew

The Passenger

Name: Lady Penelope Creighton-Ward
Age: 26
Education: Rowden, followed by finishing school in Switzerland.
Character: Stylish, sophisticated, cool under pressure.
Past duties: Before becoming International Rescue's London agent, Lady Penelope was Chief Operative of the Federal Agents Bureau.
Status: F.A.B.!

Craft and Crew

The Chauffeur

Name: Aloysius Parker
Age: 52
Education: Trained by villains in the London underworld in safe-cracking and house-burgling.
Character: Loyal, shrewd, resourceful.
Other duties include: Acting as Lady Penelope's butler and general assistant.
Status: F.A.B.!

AGENT CHALLENGE SOLUTIONS

Braman's Brain p.18

Lady Penelope Puzzles It Out! p.34
In each case the words in blue spell out INTERNATIONAL RESCUE. You could also make TERRESTRIAL CANE UNION or ENSURE CERTAIN TAN OIL, among others!

The gang's intended victims were Scott, Gordon, Tin-Tin, Brains and Alan. Here's how their names are hidden in the message:

WE WILL MEET AT ASCOT TODAY AT 2100. THE TARGETS EITHER DO NOT SUSPECT OUR GANG OR DO NOT WISH US TO KNOW THEY SUSPECT. AS A PRECAUTION, TAKE NO PART IN TINKERING WITH OUR SECRET PLANS BEFORE THE FINAL BRAIN-STORMING SESSION. THIS IS MY FINAL ANNOUNCEMENT!

Brains's Birthdays p.35
Lady Penelope's birthday is 24-12-2039. Gordon's birthday is 14-02-2043.

```
0 4 0 4 2 0 3 9 2 0
3 0 8 2 0 4 2 0 2 3
4 2 1 4 1 1 2 0 4 0
0 1 0 2 2 5 4 7 4 0
2 7 2 0 2 0 3 7 0 5
6 9 0 7 4 8 3 5 2 0
0 1 4 0 2 2 0 4 3 0
0 2 0 1 2 0 0 9 0 1
2 2 0 1 2 4 2 2 2 3
9 3 0 2 2 1 4 2 1 0
```

Pick of the Pods p.37
```
    T R U C K
  F I R E F L Y
E L E V A T O R C A R S
  E X C A V A T O R
      M O N O B R A K E
      M O L E
```

Monobrake Maze p.39

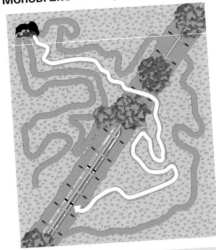

Turnaround Trouble p.52

T W O	D O M O
T O O	D O M E
T O P	H O M E
P O P	H O L E
P O D	M O L E

Transmitter Tangles p.54

```
  1      2      3      4   5
PARKERESCUEARTHELP
  6      7      8
INKYRANORBITHUNDER
  9     10
BIRDOMORANGE
```

Unidentified F.A.B. Objects! p.56
The craft in the pictures are:
Thunderbirds 1–5 and FAB 1.
In order of size, they are:
FAB 1, Thunderbird 4, Thunderbird 1, Thunderbird 2, Thunderbird 3 and Thunderbird 5.

Under Sea, Under Pressure! p.58
Cable D leads to the diving sphere.

Working for International Rescue, we are always up against the clock – and it seems that for now we are out of time. I do hope that this secret dossier has been useful to you, and that the answers on this page match your own – proving conclusively that you are a true asset to Jeff and the boys at International Rescue!

Lady Penelope Creighton-Ward